This book is dedicated to my mom, husband, and all of the special "tadpoles" in my life (Jake, Sam, Adi, Hannah, Yael, Kayla, Emma, and Max).

This book is also dedicated to all of the courageous kids out there with parents who are divorced and getting re-married to recognize that they are not alone. I am also hoping this book will be inspiring and helpful for families of mixed races, religions, and ethnicities in order to help foster a culture of acceptance and understanding that not all families look the same on the outside—which is a beautiful thing!

www.mascotbooks.com

Freeda the Frog & Her New Blue Family

For more information, please contact:
Mascot Books
560 Herndon Parkway #120
Herndon, VA 20170
info@mascotbooks.com

Library of Congress Control Number: 2016921263

CPSIA Code: PRT0317A
ISBN: 978-1-68401-132-2

Printed in the United States

Freeda the Frog
& Her New Blue Family

by Gold Mom's Choice Award winner
Nadine Haruni

art by Tina Modugno

Frannie and Frank were adjusting to their new life after their parents, Freeda and Fred, got divorced.

It was difficult to adjust at first, but Frannie and Frank soon learned to get used to going back and forth between their parents' separate lily pad homes.

They also talked to their tadpole friends (some of whose parents were also divorced), their parents, other family members, and their teachers whenever they were sad, and that helped make the transition easier.

Frogelot School

Their parents even told them that they also had trouble getting used to their new lives. All of this made Frannie and Frank feel better. They could talk about it and figure things out together.

Over time, and because they loved each other, life started to feel normal again.

Going back and forth between Freeda and Fred's lily pads was becoming fun. Frannie and Frank felt at home in both places.

On the weekends, they would often spend time with Freeda or Fred's friends, some of whom were also divorced and had their own tadpoles. It was nice to have some new tadpole friends who understood what it was like to have parents who did not live together.

One day, Freeda introduced Frannie and Frank to her new friend, Samson. Samson had a son named Jack who was about the same age as Frank. They all started spending a lot of time together on the weekends that the children were with Freeda.

Frannie noticed that Samson and Jack's skin color looked different than theirs. Samson and Jack were blue, while she, Frank, Freeda, and Fred were all green. She decided to ask Frank about it to see what he thought.

Frank told Frannie that there were lots of different colored frogs—green frogs, blue frogs, yellow frogs, red frogs, even rainbow colored frogs.

"Frogs are frogs, and tadpoles are tadpoles," he explained. "It doesn't matter what color your skin is or what you look like on the outside, we're all just frogs on the inside."

Frannie nodded. This made total sense to her.

"Besides," continued Frank, "Jack is pretty cool. We hang out a lot!"

Before long, Jack and Frank became good friends. Frank really enjoyed spending time and playing with Jack, and they soon found out that they liked doing a lot of the same things.

Frank and Jack did lots of fun activities when they were together—lily pad hopping, catching flies at the neighborhood park, having contests like who could swallow the biggest fly, and playing lots of other games. Every time Samson came over to visit Freeda on her lily pad, Jack came too so he and Frank could play.

"This is awesome," said Frank when Freeda asked him and Frannie what they thought about spending a lot of time with Samson and Jack. "We have lots of fun together!"

Hearing Frank say this was music to Freeda's frog ears.

One day when they were all together, Freeda and Samson asked Frannie, Frank, and Jack to come sit together so they could all talk.

"Samson and I have some big news we want to discuss with you," began Freeda. "This may come as a bit of a shock, but here it goes: Samson and I are not only friends, but we also love each other and we're going to get married."

Then she continued, "We know it will be hard for all of you to understand that your mommy and daddy are getting married to someone else, but this will just mean that you have a bonus parent to look out for you and love you. Samson will not be replacing your father, Frannie and Frank, and I will not be replacing your mother, Jack."

Samson chimed in, "Plus, you guys will all get to be step-tadpoles. It's an extra bonus!"

There was complete and total silence. All three tadpoles looked at each other, stunned.

Frannie and Frank went to talk alone together in Frannie's room. "This is a lot to take in," began Frannie. "I mean, we knew our parents were divorced and I guess that means they might meet someone else. *But if Mommy really marries another frog, that means it's permanent.*"

"Yeah, it's definitely weird that Mommy will be marrying someone else," replied Frank. "But Samson does make her really happy and we like him too. PLUS, Jack will be our new brother, and he's a pretty cool tadpole."

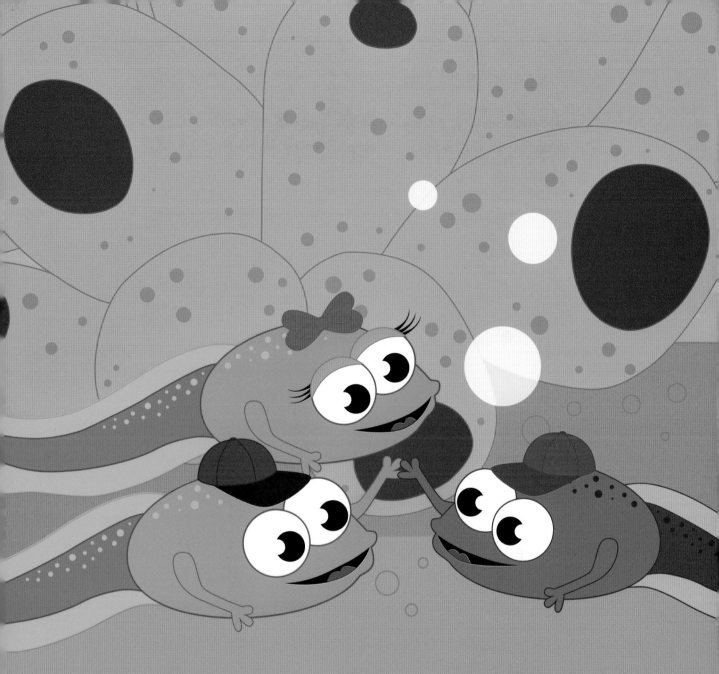

The two tadpoles thought about it for a moment before yelling, "Ribbit! Ribbit!" which is frog talk for "Woo-hoo!"

"Wait," said Frank suddenly, "I wonder what Jack thinks?"

They called Jack into Frannie's room and were overjoyed when Jack broke into a strong "Ribbit! Ribbit!" too, showing how happy he was. "We better go tell our parents!" they said together.

A few months passed and the "big day" finally arrived: wedding day! Frannie, Frank, and Jack all got to be in the wedding party, and Freeda and Samson invited their frog families and close frog friends to watch them hop down the lily pad aisle. Frannie and Frank thought it was cool that there were so many beautifully colored frogs in attendance. So cool, that they completely forgot that Samson and Jack were a different color than they were!

After Freeda and Samson exchanged wedding vows, there was a huge party to celebrate. It was a magical day for all!

After the wedding, Frannie, Frank, and Jack learned that lots of their tadpole friends at school had step-parents and tadpole siblings, and some of them even had colorful families too! Their friend Riley had a red tadpole sister, their friend Max had a yellow tadpole brother, and so on.

Everyone agreed that the only thing that matters is what's inside a frog, not what's on the outside. Families come in all sorts of colors, shapes, and sizes!

There was just one thing left that Frannie and Frank worried about. After the wedding, they would of course spend time with their dad, Fred, at his lily pad. They loved spending time with him, but felt guilty that they also really loved spending time with their new step-dad and step-brother.

They were afraid that their dad might be mad at them for being happy for their mom and her new marriage.

"What's wrong?" asked Fred, one day when Frannie and Frank were visiting and seemed a little sad. "You know you guys can tell me anything, right?"

"Um, it's nothing," said Frank, looking at Frannie. But as soon as Fred asked again, Frannie broke into tears.

"We don't want you to be upset," cried Frannie, "but we love our new step-dad and step-brother and our new colorful family. We're happy for Mommy too, but we still love you, Daddy!"

Fred immediately pulled Frannie and Frank in for a big frog family hug. "I could never be upset with either of you about this. I'm thrilled that you are both so happy in your new family, and I know Samson and Jack treat you and your mommy well, which is all I could ask for."

"You guys may have a bonus parent and a bonus brother who love you very much, but you'll always have me as your one and only frog dad," finished Fred.

Hearing those words was music to Frannie and Frank's little frog ears. Some tadpoles only get one mom frog and one dad frog. They now knew how lucky they were to have so many colorful frogs in their lives to love them. Together, they let out a loud and proud "Ribbit! Ribbit!"

The End!

Keep flipping
for more fun!

Keep up with all of the latest information about the *Freeda the Frog* books and events and order additional copies from the direct links at www.freedathefrog.com. Also be sure to follow *Freeda the Frog* on Instagram, Twitter, and Facebook!

About the Author

Nadine Haruni has gone through a divorce herself and is now re-married with five children. Her first book, *Freeda the Frog Gets a Divorce*, was awarded the *Gold Mom's Choice Award*. Nadine hopes that her second book, *Freeda the Frog & Her New Blue Family*, will be just as inspirational to other children who are coping with the difficult circumstances surrounding their parents' divorce and subsequent re-marriage. Nadine is a member of the Society of Children's Book Writers and Illustrators and the Independent Book Publishers Association. Aside from writing, she also teaches yoga to adults and kids and is a practicing attorney.

Stay tuned for Nadine's future *Freeda the Frog* books, where Freeda and the tadpoles continue to help kids face more of life's challenges.

Discussion Questions

1. What did Frannie and Frank do to help them get used to their parents being divorced?

2. Why do you think it helped make it easier for Frannie and Frank to talk to other tadpole friends whose parents were also divorced?

3. Why do you think that all three tadpoles were silent at first when Freeda told them that she and Samson were getting married?

4. Do you think Freeda was happy by how the tadpoles reacted when she told them she was getting married to Samson?

5. Would it be scary to tell your other parent that you are going to have a new step-parent? If so, why is it scary?

6. Does every family look the same?

7. What did their friends mean when they said that families "come in all different colors, shapes, and sizes"?

My Family and Our Home(s)

Draw a picture of your family and your home (or two homes, if your parents are divorced and do not live together).

Activity!
Cut along the dotted lines for your very own bookmark!

In *Freeda the Frog & Her New Blue Family*, Freeda and her family get used to life after the divorce. They have a new routine in place, but things change when Freeda meets a new blue frog and remarries. This book helps kids address their feelings when their parent remarries, and also helps foster acceptance of blended families, whether they be of mixed race, religion, or ethnicity.

ISBN: 978-1-68401-132-2

Retail Price: $14.95 US

www.freedathefrog.com